For Julia and Mason —T.S.

To Olive and Norman —R.B.

Text copyright © 2022 by Tammi Sauer
Jacket art and interior illustrations copyright © 2022 by Ross Burach

All rights reserved. Published in the United States by Doubleday, an imprint of
Random House Children's Books, a division of Penguin Random House LLC, New York.

Doubleday and the colophon are registered trademarks of Penguin Random House LLC.

Visit us on the Web! rhcbooks.com

Educators and librarians, for a variety of teaching tools,
visit us at RHTeachersLibrarians.com

Library of Congress Cataloging-in-Publication Data is available upon request.
ISBN 978-0-593-18135-5 (trade) — ISBN 978-0-593-18136-2 (lib. bdg.) —
ISBN 978-0-593-18137-9 (ebook)

MANUFACTURED IN CHINA
10 9 8 7 6 5 4 3 2 1
First Edition

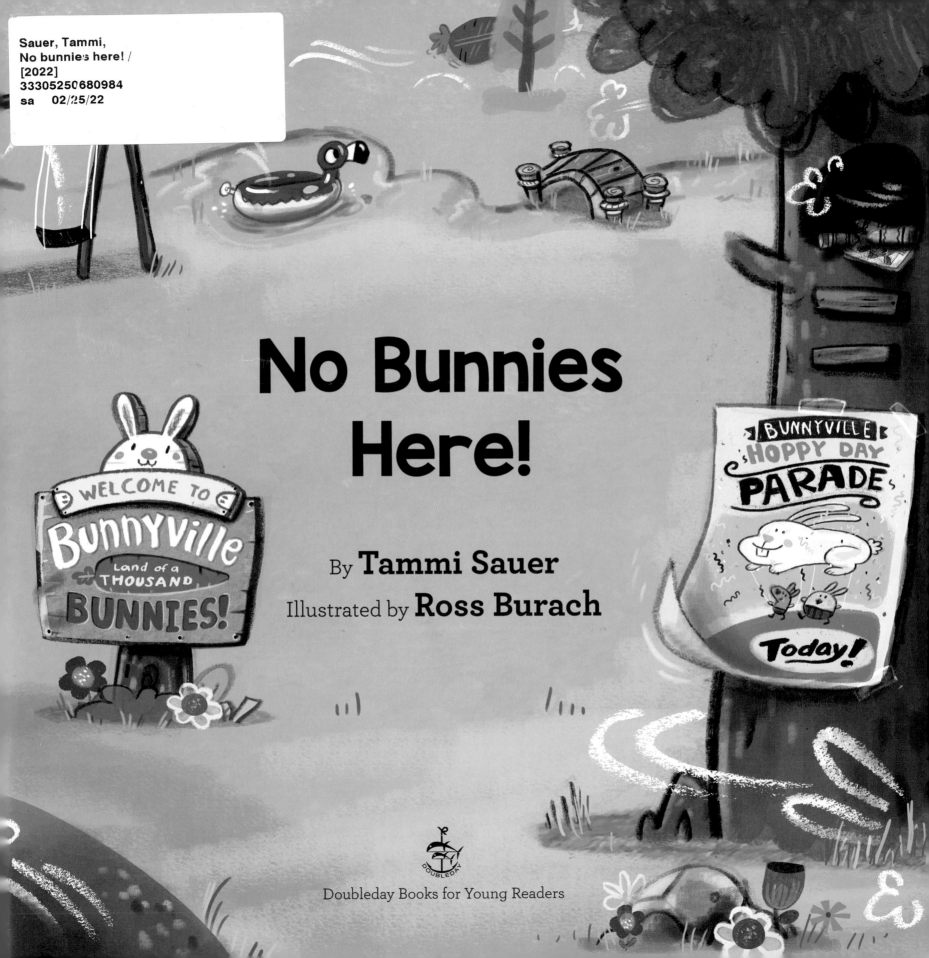

No Bunnies Here!

By **Tammi Sauer**

Illustrated by **Ross Burach**

Doubleday Books for Young Readers

Oh!

Hello there, Wolf. My, uh,
what big teeth you have.

You look–*gulp*–hungry.

Too bad there's nothing
yummy here.
Goodbye.

WELCOME TO

Bunnyville

Land of a
THOUSAND

BUNNIES!

Clearly, it's a lamp.

Heh. There are certainly lots of interesting things around this place.

Grass. That clump of dirt.
More grass. But a bunny?

Nope. There are no bunnies here.

Well! Would you look at what the wind blew our way!

Have you ever seen such a perfect pair of . . .

SQUISHY PILLOWS?

I think I'll cozy up right here
and take a nap. Nighty-night!

Oh, dear. That is definitely *not* a bunny parade.
You must be confused, Wolf.
Perhaps you just need to relax.
I know! Take a vacation!
I hear Antarctica is lovely this time of year.
Please give my regards to the penguins.

Bon voyage!
Au revoir!

Now would a bunny
speak French?
I think not.

THEN **WHY** ARE YOU TRYING SO HARD TO

FIND
A BUNNY?

You'll find a whole bunny bunch!

There are *lots* of bunnies here.